The Thief and the Housedog

When should you trust someone?

www.av2books.com

Go to **www.av2books.com**, and enter this book's unique code.

BOOK CODE

X 5 9 6 1 6

AV² by Weigl brings you media enhanced books that support active learning.

Published by AV² by Weigl
350 5th Avenue, 59th Floor New York, NY 10118
Websites: www.av2books.com   www.weigl.com

Library of Congress Cataloging-in-Publication Data

The thief and the housedog / Aesop.
    pages cm. -- (Storytime)
 Summary: "In The Thief and the Housedog, Aesop and his performers teach their audience the value of being wary of generosity. The troupe learns that trust is earned, not bought"-- Provided by publisher.
 ISBN 978-1-4896-2428-4 (hardcover : alk. paper) -- ISBN 978-1-4896-2429-1 (single user ebook) -- ISBN 978-1-4896-2430-7 (multi user ebook)
 [1. Fables. 2. Folklore.] I. Aesop.
 PZ8.2.T44 2015
 398.2--dc23
 [E]
                                    2014009671

Printed in the United States in North Mankato, Minnesota
1 2 3 4 5 6 7 8 9 0 18 17 16 15 14

052014
WEP090514

FABLE SYNOPSIS

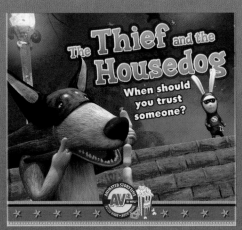

For thousands of years, parents and teachers have used memorable stories called fables to teach simple moral lessons to children.

In the Aesop's Fables by AV² series, classic fables are given a lighthearted twist. These familiar tales are performed by a troupe of animal players whose endearing personalities bring the stories to life.

In *The Thief and the Housedog*, Aesop and his performers teach their audience to be wary of being tricked. The troupe learns that trust is earned, not bought.

This AV² media enhanced book comes alive with...

Animated Video
Watch a custom animated movie.

Try This!
Complete activities and hands-on experiments.

Key Words
Study vocabulary, and complete a matching word activity.

Quiz
Test your knowledge.

The Thief and the Housedog

When should you trust someone?

AV² Storytime Navigation

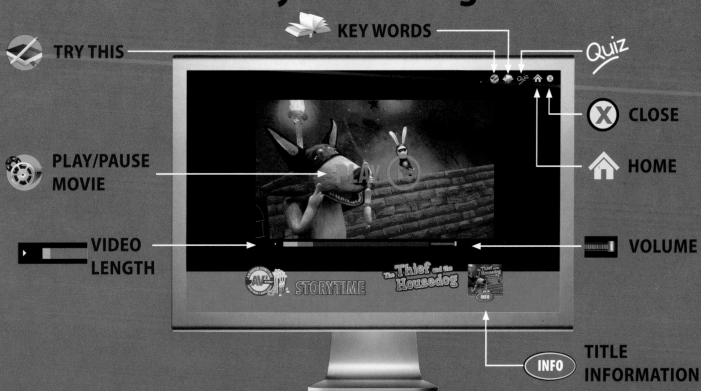

KEY WORDS

TRY THIS

Quiz

X CLOSE

PLAY/PAUSE MOVIE

HOME

VIDEO LENGTH

VOLUME

INFO TITLE INFORMATION

3

The Players

Aesop
I am the leader of Aesop's Theater, a screenwriter, and an actor.
I can be hot-tempered, but I am also soft and warm-hearted.

Libbit
I am an actor and a prop man.
I think I should have been a lion, but I was born a rabbit.

Presy
I am the manager of Aesop's Theater.
I am also the narrator of the plays.

The Story

Goddard and Audrey were walking in the forest when they saw two hyenas.

"Hello, little pigs. Would you share our dessert with us?"

The Shorties were excited.

They followed the hyenas to their picnic table.

Goddard was about to put a piece of cake into

his mouth when a hyena stopped him.

"Before you eat, would you please sign this paper?"

"If you do, we will give you a present," said another hyena.

Goddard and Audrey gladly signed the paper.

The hyenas gave each of them a present.

Goddard and Audrey returned home.

Everyone wondered who gave them the presents.

"Two nice hyenas gave them to us," said Audrey.

"What did they ask for in return?" asked Presy.

Goddard handed a piece of paper to Presy.

Goddard and Audrey's signatures were clearly written on the letter.

"Oh no!" exclaimed Presy. "This says that you owe the hyenas twenty dollars."

Aesop ran towards them.

"The hyenas gave me a present!" announced Aesop.

Did you read the piece of paper they gave you?" asked Presy.

Aesop looked at the paper in shock.

"I owe them twenty dollars?"

That evening, Aesop met with everyone.

"The hyenas gave me an idea for a new play," said Aesop.

"The play is called *The Thief and the Housedog*.

You will play the thief, Libbit. I will play the housedog."

Libbit was excited with his role.

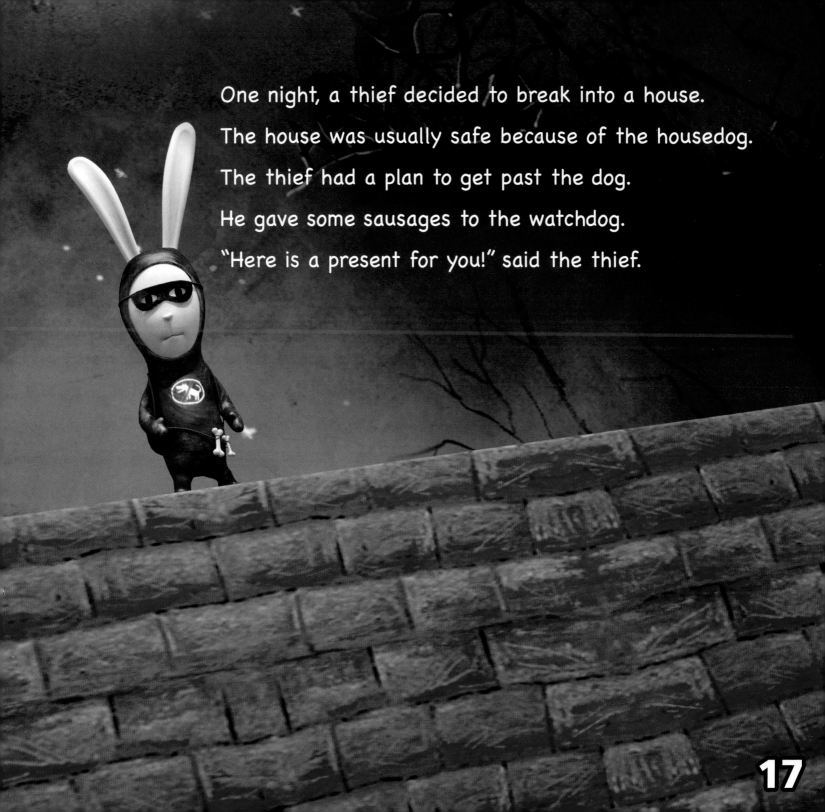

One night, a thief decided to break into a house.

The house was usually safe because of the housedog.

The thief had a plan to get past the dog.

He gave some sausages to the watchdog.

"Here is a present for you!" said the thief.

17

The housedog started eating the sausages.

The thief jumped down from the wall.

He walked slowly towards the house.

The housedog stopped eating and looked at the thief.

"Stop! Where are you going?" asked the housedog.

"Do you want more sausages?"

The thief threw another sausage at the housedog and continued towards the house.

The housedog ignored the sausage.

Instead, he barked at the thief.

"Wait!" exclaimed the thief. "I gave you food!"

"Do you think you can trick me with sausages?" said the housedog.

"I'm not going to let you steal from my master!"

The thief turned to run.

The housedog chased him.

The thief climbed up the wall.

The housedog grabbed onto his backpack.

"Please, let me go!" cried the thief.

The watchdog took the thief's backpack and let him run away.

The watchdog was pleased to find sausages inside the backpack.

"That was a great performance Libbit," said Aesop.

The Shorties cheered.

"Did you all learn your lesson?" asked Presy.

Goddard, Aubrey, and Aesop nodded.

"Let's return the presents to the hyenas," said Aesop.

"That way we won't have to pay them."

If you are too trusting, you may end up being tricked.

What is a Story?

Players

Who is the story about? The characters, or players, are the people, animals, or objects that perform the story. Characters have personality traits that contribute to the story. Readers understand how a character fits into the story by what the character says and does, what others say about the character, and how others treat the character.

Setting

Where and when do the events take place? The setting of a story helps readers visualize where and when the story is taking place. These details help to suggest the mood or atmosphere of the story. A setting is usually presented briefly, but it explains whether the story is taking place in the past, present, or future and in a large or small area.

Plot

What happens in the story? The plot is a story's plan of action. Most plots follow a pattern. They begin with an introduction and progress to the rising action of events. The events lead to a climax, which is the most exciting moment in the story. The resolution is the falling action of events. This section ties up loose ends so that readers are not left with unanswered questions. The story ends with a conclusion that brings the events to a close.

Point of View

Who is telling the story? The story is normally told from the point of view of the narrator, or storyteller. The narrator can be a main character or a less important character in the story. He or she can also be someone who is not in the story but is observing the action. This observer may be impartial or someone who knows the thoughts and feelings of the characters. A story can also be told from different points of view.

Dialogue

What type of conversation occurs in the story? Conversation, or dialogue, helps to show what is happening. It also gives information about the characters. The reader can discover what kinds of people they are by the words they say and how they say them. Writers use dialogue to make stories more interesting. In dialogue, writers imitate the way real people speak, so it is written differently than the rest of the story.

Theme

What is the story's underlying meaning? The theme of a story is the topic, idea, or position that the story presents. It is often a general statement about life. Sometimes, the theme is stated clearly. Other times, it is suggested through hints.

The Thief and the Housedog Quiz

1
What did the hyenas share with the Shorties?

2
What did Goddard and Audrey do to get presents?

3
What did Goddard and Audrey owe the hyenas?

4
Who was also tricked by the hyenas?

5
What did the thief give to the housedog?

6
What did the housedog take from the thief?

Answers:
1. Their dessert
2. Signed a piece of paper
3. Twenty dollars
4. Aesop
5. Sausages
6. His backpack

30

Key Words

Research has shown that as much as 65 percent of all written material published in English is made up of 300 words. These 300 words cannot be taught using pictures or learned by sounding them out. They must be recognized by sight. This book contains 109 common sight words to help young readers improve their reading fluency and comprehension. This book also teaches young readers several important content words, such as proper nouns. These words are paired with pictures to aid in learning and improve understanding.

Page	Sight Words First Appearance
4	a, also, am, an, and, be, been, but, can, have, I, of, plays, should, the, think, was
5	always, animals, at, do, food, from, get, good, if, like, never, other, them, to, very, want, with
6	in, little, our, saw, their, they, two, us, were, when, would, you
9	about, another, before, each, eat, give, him, his, into, paper, put, said, this, we, will
11	asked, did, for, home, no, on, that, what, who
12	me
13	read
15	idea, is, new
17	because, had, he, here, house, night, one, some
19	down, started, walked
21	are, more, stop, where
23	let, my, not, run, turned
24	away, find, go, took, up
26	all, being, end, great, learn, may, too, way, your

Page	Content Words First Appearance
4	actor, leader, lion, manager, narrator, prop man, rabbit, screenwriter, theater
5	dance, music, pig
6	dessert, forest, hyenas, picnic table
9	cake, mouth, present
11	letter, twenty dollars
15	evening, housedog, thief
17	dog, sausages
19	wall
23	master
24	backpack

Check out av2books.com for your animated storytime media enhanced book!

1. Go to av2books.com
2. Enter book code X 5 9 6 1 6
3. Fuel your imagination online!

www.av2books.com

AV² Storytime Navigation

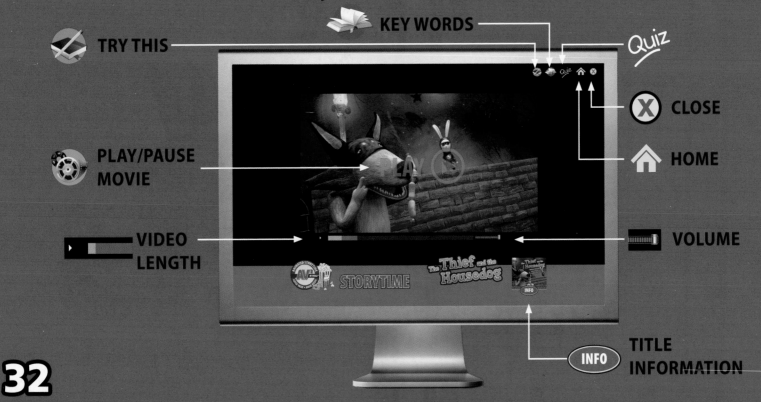

KEY WORDS

TRY THIS

Quiz

PLAY/PAUSE MOVIE

VIDEO LENGTH

X CLOSE

HOME

VOLUME

INFO TITLE INFORMATION